Brand New
BABY

Bob Graham

WALKER BOOKS
AND SUBSIDIARIES
LONDON • BOSTON • SYDNEY

Mrs Arnold was going to
have a brand new baby.
She wore dresses
as big as tents.

Edward Arnold
wore a large box.
Wendy Arnold wore her
mum's old trousers.

First published individually as
Waiting for the New Baby, Visiting the New Baby,
Bringing Home the New Baby,
and *Getting to Know the New Baby* (1989)
by Walker Books Ltd, 87 Vauxhall Walk
London SE11 5HJ

This edition published 1998

2 4 6 8 10 9 7 5 3 1

© 1989 Blackbird Design Pty Ltd
Cover illustration © 1998 Blackbird Design Pty Ltd

This book has been typeset in Monotype Bembo.

Printed in Italy

British Library Cataloguing in Publication Data
A catalogue record for this book is
available from the British Library.

ISBN 0-7445-6141-8

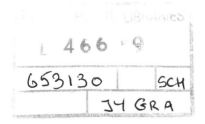

When the box
and the trousers
collided there was
trouble in the
Arnold house!

Edward cried, but it was all noise and no tears.

"Don't be so
rough with your
brother," said
Mrs Arnold.

Mum bounced Edward to help him smile again.
Then *she* needed help to get out of her chair!

Dad helped too, by ironing
the tiny clothes that
began to appear.
"They're dolls'
clothes," said Wendy.
"No, they're baby
clothes," said Dad.

Sometimes Wendy and Edward pretended that the new baby had already come.

They washed it, changed its nappy and fed it on leaves and mud and lots of watery tea.

"What shall we call the new baby when she comes?" asked Wendy. "She may be a boy," said Mum. "Oh," said Wendy. "Walter!" said Edward. "Call him Walter!"

When they sat quietly, they could
feel the new baby moving.
"It's Walter," said Wendy.
"Hello, Walter," said Edward.

And then the new baby was born. Edward and Wendy dressed up as Bat King and Wonderwoman.

Dad took them to the hospital to meet the baby for the first time.

Edward was very excited. He took his two best toys as presents for the new baby, Walter.

But baby Walter looked like he wouldn't need
toys for some time. He was very small,
and pink, and fast asleep.

"He's like a toy," said Wendy. "Will he wake up?"

"Such tiny hands," said Dad, "and he
looks like Edward."

"Where *is* Edward?"
said Dad.
"He's hiding under
the bed with his silly
presents," said Wendy.

"Come up, Edward.
Come and meet Walter
and bring your presents
with you," said Dad.

"They're much too
big for baby Walter,"
said Wendy.

"They're your best
toys! That's kind
of you, Edward,"
said Mum.

"I'm sure Walter will look at them when he wakes up.
Would you like to hold your new brother?"

"He looks like
he might break,"
said Edward.
"He's still asleep,"
said Wendy.

Edward was saved by the bell! It was time to go home.

"Are you quite sure you didn't want to hold Walter?" asked Dad, as they left the hospital.

"When he comes home," said Edward. "I'll try him when he comes home at the weekend."

On Saturday Mrs Arnold was waiting to leave the hospital with baby Walter.

Dad was still at home, busy cleaning up. He wanted everything neat and tidy for them.

Wendy and Edward weren't helping at all.

They were playing a game called "houses" and
when it was time to go to the hospital, they
were still arranging the furniture.

Wendy and Edward didn't like going to the hospital.
It smelled of medicine and floor polish.

It was nice to see Mum again, but they weren't
impressed by Walter. He didn't do anything much.

"Aren't you going
to talk to the new
baby, Edward?"
asked Dad. "You
haven't said a
word to him yet."

Edward just took his boat and his bat car because Walter didn't seem interested in them.

Mr Arnold took Mrs Arnold's bag and the nurse carried baby Walter. Wendy thought Walter looked a bit like a sleeping prune.

On the bus, Walter
suddenly woke up.

He struggled and
curled his fingers.

His face changed
colour, and he
burped very loudly.

"Wow!" said Wendy.
"Not bad!" said Edward.

It was the most
interesting thing
Walter had ever done!

When they got home, Grandma was waiting to help with the baby. "Anyone for tea and cake?" she said.
"Not for the baby!" said Edward.
"Not for Walter," said Wendy. "He's just made the biggest burp you've ever heard!"

The trouble with
Walter was that Mum
and Dad never had
time for anything else.

They managed to
find time to bath him
and watch him kick
and suck his fists …

but they had no time
to help with pyjamas,
the way they used to.

In fact, Mum was
always feeding
the baby …

or washing or ironing or sleeping.

She fell asleep
a lot when she
wasn't with
baby Walter.

Baby Walter slept a lot too.

So games had to be played very, very quietly,

even when they were very, very

exciting.

But when Edward and his sister were in *their* beds
and fast asleep, Walter could wake up and make as
much noise as he liked … or so it seemed.

In the mornings
Walter was much
more likeable.
Wendy and
Edward slowly
got used to their
baby brother.

They even helped
when he needed
his nappy changed.

And every day Walter did new things.

Some days, he
looked at Wendy
and Edward
and smiled as if
he knew who
they were.

At last Mum and Dad had more
time to play games.

And baby Walter almost seemed
part of the family!